Anna Achoo!

'Anna Achoo!'
An original concept by Jenny Moore
© Jenny Moore 2022

Illustrated by Katie Crumpton

Published by MAVERICK ARTS PUBLISHING LTD
Studio 11, City Business Centre, 6 Brighton Road,
Horsham, West Sussex, RH13 5BB
© Maverick Arts Publishing Limited February 2022
+44 (0)1403 256941

A CIP catalogue record for this book is available at the British Library.

ISBN 978-1-84886-860-1

Maverick
publishing

www.maverickbooks.co.uk

White

This book is rated as: White Band (Guided Reading)

Anna Achoo!

by Jenny Moore

illustrated by Katie Crumpton

Chapter 1

Ghost Anna's house had been empty for years. There were cracks in the windows and holes in the roof. The back door was broken. Everything inside was covered in dust and cobwebs, and everything outside was covered in ivy and weeds. The garden looked like a jungle.

Anna wept ghostly tears as she looked at the faded FOR SALE sign. She could just see the top of it sticking out of a tall patch of stinging nettles. Anna longed for a new family to move

in and share her house. It was lonely being a
ghost. She wanted to be around living people
again. She wanted to watch television with
them. She wanted to read books over their
shoulders and laugh at their jokes. But no one
wanted to buy a haunted house.

Anna had tried hiding when families came to
look around. But she couldn't hide her sneezes.

Achoo! There was so much dust on the carpets!
Every time someone walked across the floor,
the clouds of dust made Anna sneeze. Achoo!
Achoo! Achoo! And a few ghostly sneezes were
enough to send the family running out of the
house, screaming.

Chapter 2

One day, Anna spotted a boy standing on the street corner. He was staring up at the house.

'Perhaps he's seen the FOR SALE sign,' she thought. 'Maybe he and his family are looking for somewhere to live...'

"This could be my big chance," Anna told herself, wiping away her tears. "I just need to find a way to stop sneezing."

Anna remembered the old
dustpan and brush she'd
seen in the attic. "That's it!"
she cried. "If I sweep all the
dust away then it can't tickle my nose!"

She floated up through the bedroom ceiling into
the attic. It was years since she'd been up here.

All the old boxes of toys in the attic usually
made her feel sad. But not today. Today Anna
scanned the attic, looking for the dustpan and
brush. Yes! There it was! But when Anna tried
to pick it up, her hands passed straight through
the handle.

"Bother!" She tried again and again.

But it was no good. Her wispy ghost fingers couldn't grip it properly.

Anna refused to give up though. "There's got to be another way," she told the spider scuttling along the attic beam. "Hmm. If I can't sweep the dust away, maybe I can blow it away, instead."

Chapter 3

Back downstairs, Anna took a deep breath in
and blew. She puffed out a tiny breath, but it
wasn't strong enough to do anything. The layer
of dust on the hall radiator was just as thick
as before. She took an even deeper breath and
tried again. It was no good though. The dust
stayed exactly where it was.

"Come on," Anna told herself firmly. "You
can do this." She took an even bigger breath,
sucking in as much air as she could.

Then she shut her eyes, puffed out her cheeks, and blew. A ticklish cloud of dust flew up Anna's nose making her sneeze.

Achoo!

Her eyes began to water as the sneezes grew bigger and bigger.

Achoo!
ACHOO!
ACHOO!

"Oh no," she cried between sneezes.
"I don't think that was such
a good idea after all!"

ACHOO!

Anna dived through the
wall into the kitchen,
trying to escape the
tickling dust.

ACHOO! ACHOO!

"AHHHH!" came a loud scream.

Anna spun round to see a boy!

"Oh!" cried Anna in surprise. "I'm sorry,"
she said. "I didn't mean to frighten you!"

The boy backed away towards the door.
His cheeks were pale and his legs were shaking.
"P-please don't hurt me," he whispered.

"Of course I won't," said Anna. "I'd never hurt
anyone. I'm just a bit allergic to dust, that's
all." She sneezed again.

"B-but you're a g-ghost," stammered the boy.

"Yes," admitted Anna. "I'm a nice ghost though,
I promise. Please don't go."

Chapter 4

The boy looked a little less scared now.
He looked a bit less pale too.

"I'm allergic to grass pollen," he said. "But dust
doesn't bother me at all. I'm Kai," he added.

"And I'm Anna a-a-achoo!"

Kai smiled. "Anna Achoo? That's a funny name.
I'm looking for a grey cat called Gertie. I
thought she might have sneaked into this house.

Have you seen her?"

Anna shook her head. "I'm afraid not. But if she is in the house, I can help you find her. It'll be nice to have some company for a change," she added. "I get very lonely here on my own."

"I know the feeling," said Kai. "I left all my old friends behind when we moved. I don't know anyone here yet except for Gertie! That's why I'm trying to find her."

"I could be your friend if you'd like," said Anna.

"If you don't mind having a sneezing ghost for a friend."

"A ghost friend would be cool! I'd love to be able to walk through walls and make people jump!"

"Really?" said Anna. "I'd just like to be able to hold a dustpan and brush so I can get rid of all this dust. Maybe then someone will finally want to buy my house."

"I could help with that," Kai offered. "I'll pop back to our flat for the vacuum cleaner. That'll be quicker than a dustpan – and less dusty too! And then you can show me some more ghost tricks when I've finished."

"It's a deal!" Anna agreed, happily. "Ahhh!" she cried, as something grey and furry shot across the kitchen floor. "What was that?"

"Gertie!" laughed Kai. "I've found you!"

Chapter 5

Kai came back every day that week to help clean the house.

Kai vacuumed and cleaned and polished, while Anna showed off her best ghost tricks and told him stories about all the different people who'd lived in the house.

"No one's lived here for years now though," she said. "As soon as someone comes to look round, I scare them off with my sneezing."

"You're not sneezing anymore though," Kai pointed out. "Maybe it will be different now the house is all nice and clean again." He stared round at the sparkling surfaces. "In fact, maybe I should bring Mum and Dad round to have a look at it. We've got to move out of our flat soon. We've been looking for somewhere to buy, but all the houses are too expensive."

Anna's eyes shone with excitement. "This is the cheapest house in town. They keep knocking extra money off the price because it's haunted!"

Kai grinned. "Dad's a builder so he'll be able to do all the repairs himself."

"Perfect!" said Anna. "And once you move in, we'll be able to watch television and read books together every night! I just need to stay hidden and hold in my sneezes when your mum and dad come to look round. Operation 'Quiet Ghost' here we come!"

But by the time Kai and his parents arrived with the estate agent that weekend, Anna was starting to worry. Would she be able to keep to the plan? Her nose was tickling already...

Chapter 6

"And here we have the sitting room," said the estate agent.

Anna watched from behind the curtains, trying not to breathe. The tickle in her nose was growing though.

"This is great," said Kai. "Don't you think? Gertie would love it here. It might stop her running away all the time!"

His mum nodded. "Very nice. The lady in the post office told me it was haunted though. She said that's why it's so cheap."

"Haunted?" said Kai. "Don't be silly!"

"There's no such thing as ghosts," agreed Kai's dad. "It's just an old house in need of a few repairs. I bet there's a nice wooden floor under this carpet." He pulled back the loose edge of

the carpet, sending a big cloud of dust up into the air.

A-a-a-choo! Achoo! ACHOO! ACHOO!

Kai's mum gasped. "Agh! What was that? It must be the ghost!"

'Oh no!' thought Anna miserably. 'I've blown it now.'

"No, that was me," said Kai, winking at Anna. "It's all the grass pollen in the garden. It must have set my allergies off again."

Kai's mum relaxed. "Of course. Silly me," she said.

Operation 'Quiet Ghost' was a success, thanks to Kai's quick thinking. His parents bought the house and they all moved in a few months later.

It looked very different by the time Kai's dad had finished his repairs though.

There were new tiles on the roof, new crack-free windows and the back door was mended. Now that the carpets had been taken up there was a lot less dust too.

Anna hardly sneezed at all anymore. And when she did, Kai always pretended it was him... even in winter.

"I must be coming down with a cold," he'd say, with a wink.

The End

Book Bands for Guided Reading

Pink

Red

Yellow

Blue

Green

Orange

Turquoise

Purple

Gold

White

The Institute of Education book banding system is a scale of colours that reflects the various levels of reading difficulty. The bands are assigned by taking into account the content, the language style, the layout and phonics. Word, phrase and sentence level work is also taken into consideration.

Maverick Early Readers are a bright, attractive range of books covering the pink to white bands. All of these books have been book banded for guided reading to the industry standard and edited by a leading educational consultant.

To view the whole Maverick Readers scheme, visit our website at www.maverickearlyreaders.com

Or scan the QR code above to view our scheme instantly!